I SPY DINOSAURS!

Before you begin
to spy dinosaurs,
learn their names
from **A** to **Z** in the
last page.

GOOD LUCK!

I SPY with my little eye, something beginning with...

A is for

Ankylosaurus!

I SPY with my little eye, something beginning with...

B

B is for Brachiosaurus!

I SPY with my little eye, something beginning with...

C is for Ceratosaurus!

I SPY with my little eye, something beginning with...

D is for
Dilophosaurus!

I SPY with my little eye, something beginning with...

E is for

Elasmosaurus!

I SPY with my little eye, something beginning with...

F is for Fukuiraptor!

I SPY with my little eye, something beginning with...

G is for Gallimimus!

I SPY with my little eye, something beginning with...

H is for Hypsilophodon!

I SPY with my little eye, something beginning with...

I

is for

Iguanodon!

I SPY with my little eye, something beginning with...

J

J

is for

Jaxartosaurus!

I SPY with my little eye, something beginning with...

K

K is for Kentrosaurus!

I SPY with my little eye, something beginning with...

L

is for

Lambeosaurus!

I SPY with my little eye, something beginning with...

M

M

is for

Mamenchisaurus!

I SPY with my little eye, something beginning with...

N

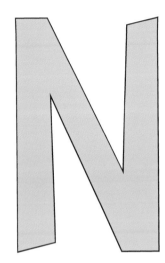 is for

Nodosaurus!

I SPY with my little eye, something beginning with...

O is for Olorotitan!

I SPY with my little eye, something beginning with...

P is for
Parasaurolophus!

I SPY with my little eye, something beginning with...

Q is for

Quaesitosaurus!

I SPY with my little eye, something beginning with...

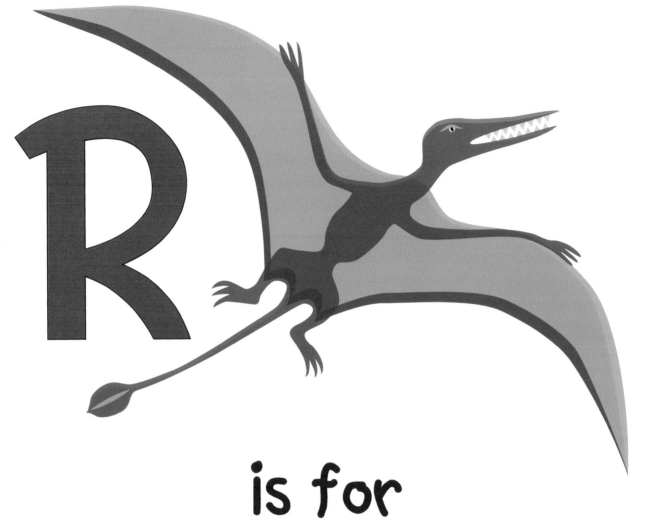

is for

Rhamphorhynchus!

I SPY with my little eye, something beginning with...

S is for Spinosaurus!

I SPY with my little eye, something beginning with...

T is for

Tyrannosaurus
Rex (T-Rex)

I SPY with my little eye, something beginning with...

U is for Utahceratops!

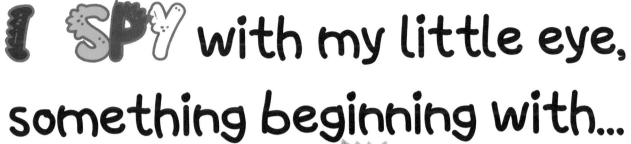 with my little eye, something beginning with...

V

is for

Velociraptor!

I SPY with my little eye, something beginning with...

W is for

Wuerhosaurus!

I SPY with my little eye, something beginning with...

X is for Xenoceratops!

I SPY with my little eye, something beginning with...

y is for Yunguisaurus!

I SPY with my little eye, something beginning with...

Z
is for

Zuniceratops!

DINOSAUR ALPHABET

ANKYLOSAURUS   **B**RACHIOSAURUS   **C**ERATOSAURUS   **D**ILOPHOSAURUS   **E**LASMOSAURUS

FUKUIRAPTOR   **G**ALLIMIMUS   **H**YPSILOPHODON   **I**GUANODON   **J**AXARTOSAURUS

KENTROSAURUS   **L**AMBEOSAURUS   **M**AMENCHISAURUS   **N**ODOSAURUS   **O**LOROTITAN

PARASAUROLOPHUS   **Q**UAESITOSAURUS   **R**HAMPHORHYNCHUS   **S**PINOSAURUS   **T**-REX   **U**TAHCERATOPS

VELOCIRAPTOR   **W**UERHOSAURUS   **X**ENOCERATOPS   **Y**UNGUISAURUS   **Z**UNICERATOPS

Printed in Great Britain
by Amazon